Funny Bone Readers

Helping Others

Mr. Mouse's Motel

by Jeff Dinardo • illustrated by Peter Lubach

Please visit our website at **www.redchairpress.com**.
Find a free catalog of all our high-quality products for young readers.

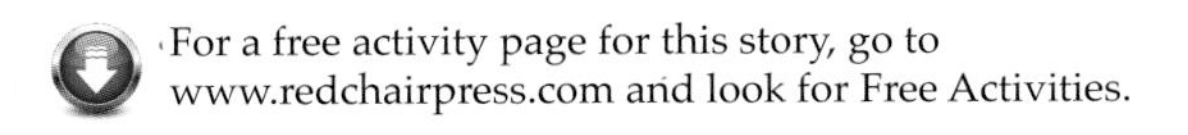
For a free activity page for this story, go to
www.redchairpress.com and look for Free Activities.

Mr. Mouse's Motel: Helping Others

Publisher's Cataloging-In-Publication Data
(Prepared by The Donohue Group, Inc.)

Dinardo, Jeffrey.

Mr. Mouse's Motel : helping others / by Jeff Dinardo ; illustrated by Peter Lubach.
p. : col. ill. ; cm. -- (Funny bone readers)
Summary: Mr. Mouse likes helping others, but what happens when Mr. Mouse get worn out? The guests at Mr. Mouse's Motel help young readers learn that it's best to share responsibilities and help others. Book features: Big Words and Big Questions.
Interest age level: 004-006.
ISBN: 978-1-939656-17-9 (lib. binding/hardcover)
ISBN: 978-1-939656-05-6 (pbk.)
ISBN: 978-1-939656-24-7 (ebook)
1. Helping behavior--Juvenile fiction. 2. Motels--Juvenile fiction. 3. Mice--Juvenile fiction. 4. Helpfulness--Fiction. 5. Hotels, motels, etc.--Fiction. 6. Mice--Fiction. I. Lubach, Peter. II. Title.
PZ7.D6115 Mr 2014

[E] 2013937169

This series first published by:
Red Chair Press LLC PO Box 333 South Egremont, MA 01258-0333

Printed in the United States of America

1 2 3 4 5 18 17 16 15 14

Mr. Mouse owns a motel.
He runs it all by himself.
It is a very tidy place.

Today there is a convention in town.
The motel is filled with guests.

The line is long to check in.

Mr. Mouse works very hard.
He signs everyone in.
He carries suitcases.
He hands out room keys.

Now everything is quiet again.
Mr. Mouse can rest.

Suddenly the phone rings.
"RING, RING. RING, RING."

"May I help you?" asks Mr. Mouse.
It was the guest in room 1.
"Can I have some ice please?"
said the guest.
Mr. Mouse brings a bucket of ice.

Then, the phone rings again.
"RING, RING. RING, RING."

It was the guest in room 2.
"May I please have extra pillows?"
asks the guest.
Mr. Mouse brings the pillows.

The phone keeps ringing!
The guest in room 3 wants a cold drink.
The guest in room 4 says his room is hot.
The guest in room 5 wants something to eat.
The guest in room 6 wants a book to read.

The phone keeps ringing!
The guest in room 7 needs help with the TV.
The guest in room 8 lost her room key.
And the guest in room 9 just wants to talk.

8

Mr. Mouse is very tired!
The phone keeps ringing but he does not answer it. It rings and rings.

The guests come to the lobby
to see what is wrong.
They see Mr. Mouse.
They know they have to help.

They bring Mr. Mouse a comfy chair.
They get him a cozy blanket and slippers.
They give him lemonade and a good book.

Then the guests finally rest.
They are tired too.
"Is there anything else we
can get you?" they ask.

But Mr. Mouse does not answer.
He is fast asleep.

Big Questions: Why was Mr. Mouse so tired? Do you think the guests were mean to Mr. Mouse? What did the guests do to make Mr. Mouse feel better?

Big Words:

convention: a big meeting

guest: one who visits a place and is welcomed there

motel: a place where one can sleep away from home